SPORTS SUPERSTARS

MOOKIE BETTS

By Derek Moon

Kaleidoscope
Minneapolis, MN

Your Front Row Seat to the Games

This edition is co-published by agreement between Kaleidoscope and World Book, Inc.

Kaleidoscope Publishing, Inc.
6012 Blue Circle Drive
Minnetonka, MN 55343 U.S.A.

World Book, Inc.
180 North LaSalle St., Suite 900
Chicago IL 60601 U.S.A.

Kaleidoscope ISBNs
978-1-64519-044-8 (library bound)
978-1-64494-201-7 (paperback)
978-1-64519-145-2 (ebook)

World Book ISBN
978-0-7166-4348-7 (library bound)

Library of Congress Control Number
2019940063

Printed in the United States of America.

TABLE OF CONTENTS

CHAPTER 1

World Series Bound

Mookie Betts got into position in right field. He set his feet. His eyes focused in on the play that was about to begin. The Boston Red Sox pitcher began his windup. Houston Astros batter Tony Kemp bent his knees. In came the pitch. Crack!

"It's a base hit by Kemp," the announcer called out.

There was one problem for Kemp. Betts was on the move. And he was running fast. The ball rolled toward the right field corner. Betts fielded it on the run. Quickly he spun around. Betts wrapped his fingers around the ball. He drove forward with his right leg. Then he whipped his arm. The ball flew out like a laser. He knew he needed to make a play. A trip to the World Series was on the line.

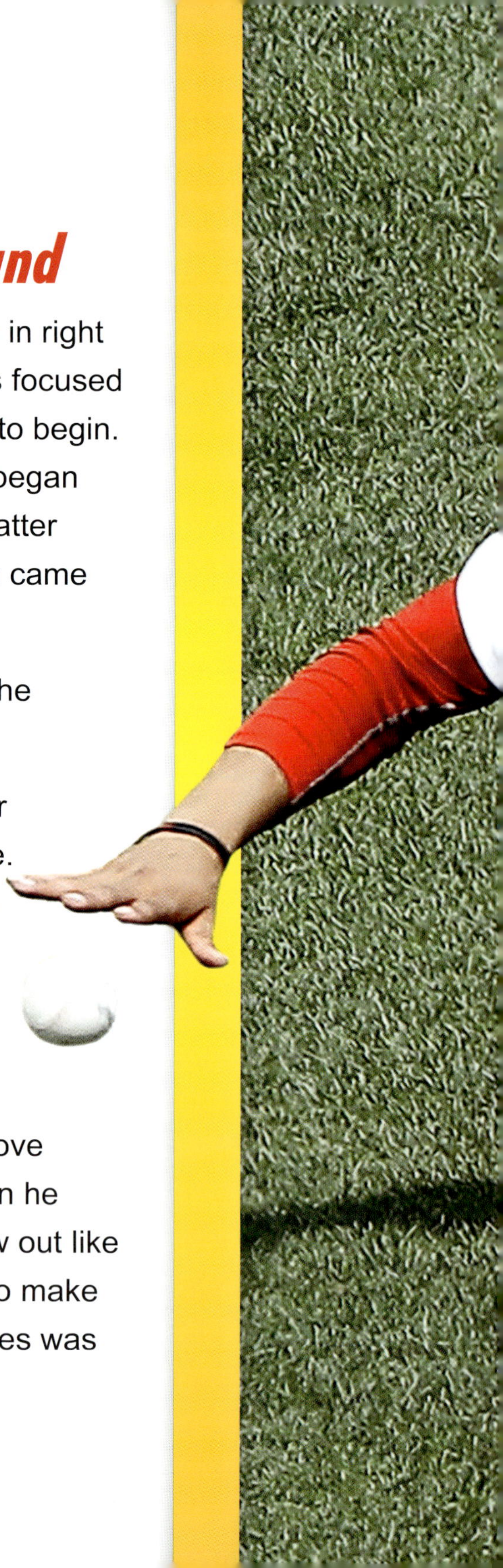

Runners must beware when Mookie Betts is in the outfield.

Betts has good speed and a strong arm.

Kemp had rounded first. He raced to second as fast as he could. Then he dove headfirst. It was too late. Betts's throw was right on target. With a quick tag by the shortstop, Kemp was out. The Red Sox star outfielder had come through once again.

Betts was 26 at the time. That was younger than average for Major League Baseball (MLB) players. Yet Betts was already an all-around star. That showed with plays like this in the 2018 **playoffs**.

WHO IS MOOKIE?

Diana Benedict turned on the TV. Basketball was on. One player stood out. His name was Mookie Blaylock. Diana liked the name. It also sounded similar to her sister, Cookie. Diana decided it was a good nickname for Markus, her newborn son. He's been called Mookie Betts ever since.

CAREER
STATS

Through the 2018 season

GAMES PLAYED	644
BATTING AVERAGE	.303
RUNS BATTED IN (RBIs)	390
HOME RUNS	110
STOLEN BASES	110

But at the plate, Betts was in a **slump**. Hits he usually got weren't coming. So Betts made sure to focus hard on his other skills. Against Kemp, he read the play quickly. He took a perfect path. Then he threw the ball super hard. The play was important. It helped Boston win the game. One day later, they won again. They made the World Series.

They went on to beat the Los Angeles Dodgers. Betts was not at his best in the playoffs. But he was still able to help his team. That's what a superstar does.

Betts hits a home run in Game 5 of the 2018 World Series.

CHAPTER 2

Small Kid, Big Heart

Mookie Betts was excited. He and his mom arrived at a school. But they weren't there to study. It was time to sign up for Little League. Mookie was five. He was an active kid. He was always moving. Now he wanted to play baseball.

Mookie and his mom approached a coach. The coach looked at Mookie. He was short for his age. The coach thought for a moment. Then he said no. Mookie was too short. The coach wanted bigger kids. This bummed Mookie out. "Nobody wants to have me," he said.

His mom, Diana Benedict, had other ideas. She set up her own team.

FUN FACT
Betts's uncle is former MLB player Terry Shumpert.

Like a lot of kids, Mookie started out playing Little League baseball.

Mookie can handle both kinds of strikes as a bowler and baseball player.

Diana knew Mookie had talent. He was born October 7, 1992. Mookie grew up near Nashville, Tennessee. His parents, Diana and Willie, split when Mookie was ten. But they supported their son. When Mookie wanted to play sports, his parents made sure he could.

Baseball came naturally to Mookie. After his first year, Mookie never again had trouble finding a team. Other sports were easy for Mookie, too. He could roll **strikes** at the bowling alley. He could swish basketball shots. He even beat all his friends at ping-pong.

Mookie played three sports in high school. Basketball was his winter sport. Mookie played point guard. It's an important position. Mookie understood the game well. This helped him set up plays. Mookie was also on the school bowling team. But he loved the spring. That was baseball season.

Mookie was fast. He hustled. He also had great skills. As a senior, he batted .549. More than half of his at-bats became hits. Mookie wanted to play college baseball next. Many teams wanted him. But pro teams wanted him, too. In 2011, the Red Sox called. They had picked Mookie in the MLB **Draft**.

FUN FACT

Betts originally planned to play college baseball at the University of Tennessee. But he changed his mind when the Red Sox drafted him.

Mookie hits in an instructional league game in 2011.

CHAPTER 3

Fans line up hoping to get Betts's autograph at spring training in 2016.

A Player Who Cares

It was late. Mookie Betts should have been tired. Game 2 of the 2018 World Series had just ended. Betts's big plays helped the Red Sox win. But he wasn't going home. He didn't go out to celebrate either.

At 1:00 a.m., Betts pulled up his hoodie. Then he started pushing. The shopping cart was heavy. It was filled with food. Betts and his cousin pushed the food to the Boston Public Library. Many homeless people were sleeping outside. Betts didn't want them to go hungry.

Dozens of hungry people got to eat that night. But Betts didn't want attention. He didn't tell anybody. He had even tried to cover his face with his hoodie. But people still recognized him. Soon everyone knew what he had done.

Baseball is important to Betts. So is being a good person off the field. But not many people know about Betts's personality. He likes to stay low-key.

Family plays a big role in Betts's life. In middle school, he saw a girl. Her name was Brianna Hammonds. Soon they started dating. They never stopped. Betts and Hammonds got **engaged**. On November 6, 2018, their family grew. Hammonds gave birth to a daughter!

FUN FACT

Betts's middle name is Lynn. His mom chose that so his initials would be MLB.

WHAT A BOWLER!

Betts lines up. He stares at his target. Then he winds up and delivers. The baseball star isn't hitting a home run. He's rolling a strike. Betts began bowling at age three. Now he's really good. Sometimes he plays on the pro tour. He's even bowled perfect games!

Betts waves to fans at the Red Sox World Series parade in 2018.

When he's not playing baseball, Betts stays busy. He spends time with family. He plays other sports. He also gives back to others. In 2017, he hosted an event. It was called Mookie's Big League Bowl. Many people came. Some were **celebrities** like Betts. Together they raised money. It went to help local families.

"I like being somebody people look up to," Betts said.

Betts wears pink gear in 2018 to promote breast cancer research.

CAREER TIMELINE

1992

October 7, 1992
Markus Lynn "Mookie" Betts is born in Tennessee.

2011

June 7, 2011
The Boston Red Sox select Betts in the fifth round of the MLB Draft.

2014

June 29, 2014
Betts makes his major league debut. He goes 1-for-3 as the Red Sox beat the Yankees.

2016

July 12, 2016
Betts plays in his first All-Star Game.

2017

November 12, 2017
Betts bowls a perfect game in the World Series of Bowling professional tournament.

2018

October 24, 2018
Betts and the Red Sox beat the Los Angeles Dodgers in Game 2 of the World Series. Hours later, Betts delivers food to homeless people in Boston.

2018

October 28, 2018
Betts and the Red Sox beat the Dodgers to win the World Series.

2018

November 6, 2018
Betts becomes a father when his fiancée gives birth to a baby girl.

2018

November 15, 2018
Betts is named American League Most Valuable Player after hitting .346 with 80 RBIs and 32 home runs.

CHAPTER 4

Betts fields the ball as a shortstop for the Lowell Spinners in 2011.

The Next Red Sox Star

Mookie Betts dug his feet in the dirt. He held the bat tight. But maybe it was too tight. A pitch blazed across the plate. Betts swung and missed. Strikeout. The summer of 2012 was hard for Betts. He was in Lowell, Massachusetts. His **minor league** team played there. But being so far from home was hard. Betts hit only .267.

No one knew what to make of Betts. The Red Sox had drafted him. But 171 players were picked before him. He wasn't a top **prospect**. Betts considered going to college instead. But the Red Sox offered him $750,000. He took it. Now he had to prove himself in the minors.

FUN FACT

Betts played infield for most of his minor league career. But he has usually been an outfielder with the Red Sox.

Betts began the 2013 season with a team in South Carolina. It was a higher level of the minor leagues. But it was closer to home. Betts felt more comfortable. It showed. He began to play like a rising star.

There was only one problem. Betts played shortstop. And the Red Sox had a good shortstop.

Betts celebrates with teammate Stephen Drew after the Red Sox win in his major league debut.

Betts decided to switch positions. Outfield was the best fit. Betts studied being an outfielder. Before long, he was a star there, too. Betts could do it all. The Red Sox kept moving him to higher levels. He faced tougher competition. By June 2014, he was ready. The Red Sox called him up to the majors.

Where Betts Has Been

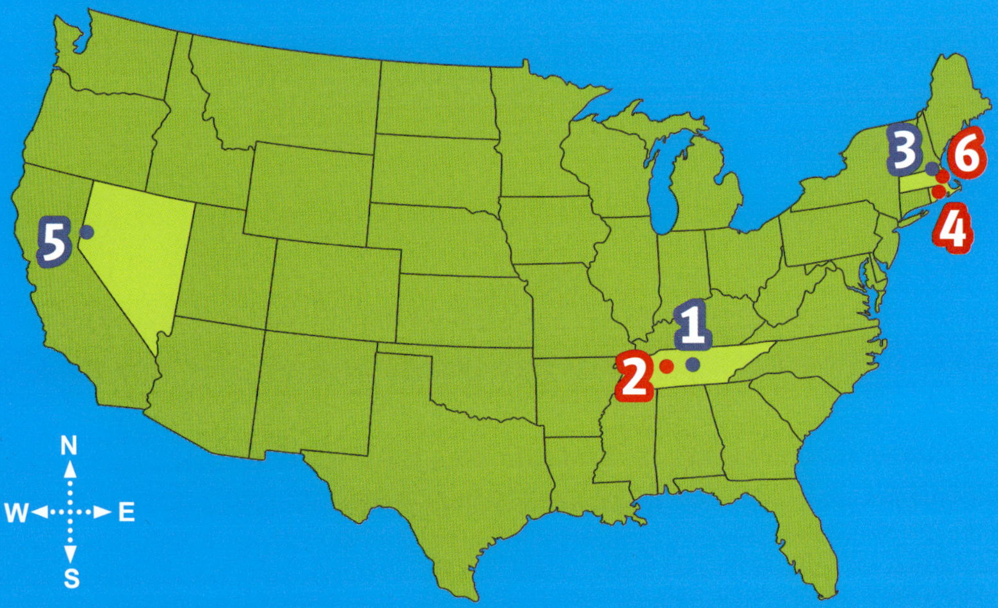

1 **Murfreesboro, Tennessee:** Where Betts lived until age 10.

2 **Brentwood, Tennessee:** Where Betts moved at age 10.

3 **Lowell, Massachusetts:** Where Betts played his first full minor league season in 2012 with the Red Sox's Single-A team.

4 **Pawtucket, Rhode Island:** Where Betts played Triple-A baseball in 2014.

5 **Reno, Nevada:** Where Betts bowled a perfect game in the PBA World Series of Bowling.

6 **Boston, Massachusetts:** Where Betts plays with the Red Sox.

Lights shined down on Yankee Stadium. Nearly 50,000 fans looked on. At age 21, Betts stepped to the plate. He got into position. *Smack!* A hard ground ball rolled into the outfield. Betts had his first major league hit. Then he tried to steal second. Too slow. Betts was out. But the play showed off his **aggressive** style.

Betts was a regular in 2015. By 2016, he was a star. Betts stands 5-foot-9 (1.75 m). He weighs 180 pounds (82 kg). Many players are bigger. But Betts does things they can't. Betts is fast. He can steal bases or rob hits. He can hit, too. Betts even blasted 32 homers in 2018. Nobody in the American League (AL) was better. At age 26, he led the Red Sox. They won the World Series. Then he was named AL Most Valuable Player (MVP). Betts had arrived.

Teammates pour water on Betts to celebrate his game-winning home run in a 2018 game.

BEYOND THE BOOK

After reading the book, it's time to think about what you learned. Try the following exercises to jumpstart your ideas.

THINK

THAT'S NEWS TO ME. Chapter Three talked about Mookie Betts delivering food to the homeless. How might news sources be able to fill in more detail about this? What new information could you find in news articles? Where could you go to find those sources?

CREATE

PRIMARY SOURCES. A primary source is an original document, photograph, or interview. Make a list of different primary sources you might be able to find about Mookie Betts. What new information might you learn from these sources?

SHARE

SUM IT UP. Write one paragraph summarizing the important points from this book. Make sure it's in your own words. Don't just copy what is in the text. Share the paragraph with a classmate. Does your classmate have any comments about the summary? Do they have additional questions about Mookie Betts?

GROW

REAL-LIFE RESEARCH. What places could you visit to learn more about Mookie Betts? What other things could you learn while you were there?

RESEARCH NINJA

Visit www.ninjaresearcher.com/0448 to learn how to take your research skills and book report writing to the next level!

RESEARCH

DIGITAL LITERACY TOOLS

SEARCH LIKE A PRO

Learn about how to use search engines to find useful websites.

FACT OR FAKE?

Discover how you can tell a trusted website from an untrustworthy resource.

TEXT DETECTIVE

Explore how to zero in on the information you need most.

SHOW YOUR WORK

Research responsibly—learn how to cite sources.

WRITE

GET TO THE POINT

Learn how to express your main ideas.

PLAN OF ATTACK

Learn prewriting exercises and create an outline.

DOWNLOADABLE REPORT FORMS

Further Resources

BOOKS

Bates, Greg. *Mookie Betts*. Focus Readers, 2019.

Jacobs, Greg. *The Everything Kids' Baseball Book: From Baseball's History to Today's Favorite Players—With Lots of Home Run Fun in Between!* 10th ed. Adams Media, 2018.

Kelley, K. C. *Boston Red Sox*. AV2 by Weigl, 2018.

WEBSITES

FACTSURFER

Factsurfer.com gives you a safe, fun way to find more information.

1. Go to www.factsurfer.com.
2. Enter "Mookie Betts" into the search box and click .
3. Select your book cover to see a list of related websites.

Glossary

aggressive: When players take risks with the hope for more rewards, they are playing an aggressive style. Mookie Betts is an aggressive player.

celebrities: Celebrities are people who are famous. The players on the Red Sox are celebrities.

draft: Sports teams use a draft to choose new players to play for them. Betts was taken in the fifth round of the MLB Draft.

engaged: People become engaged when they agree to get married. Betts got engaged in 2018.

minor league: A level of pro baseball in which players progress up the levels to MLB is called a minor league. Each major league team has its own minor league teams.

playoffs: The playoffs, in which teams compete for the championship, take place after the regular season. The 2018 Red Sox made the playoffs.

prospect: A prospect is a young baseball player who has not yet established himself in the major leagues. Betts was not considered a top prospect at first.

slump: When a baseball player performs below his usual expectations, he is said to be in a slump. Betts experienced a slump during the 2018 playoffs.

strikes: In bowling, strikes happen when a player knocks over all ten pins on the first roll. Mookie Betts gets a lot of strikes when bowling.

Index

PHOTO CREDITS

The images in this book are reproduced through the courtesy of: Winslow Townson/AP Images, front cover (center), pp. 4–5; David J. Phillip/AP Images, front cover (right), pp. 3, 8; EFKS/Shutterstock Images, front cover (background top); Marcio Jose Bastos Silva/Shutterstock Images, front cover (background bottom), p. 5; Kathy Willens/AP Images, pp. 6, 24–25; Kyodo/AP Images, p. 9; Dan Thornberg/Shutterstock Images, p. 10; tammykayphoto/Shutterstock Images, p. 11; George Rudy/Shutterstock Images, pp. 12–13; Jason Kolenda/Shutterstock Images, pp. 13, 21 (map); LunaseeStudios/Shutterstock Images, pp. 14, 21 (hat); Mike Janes/Four Seam Images/AP Images, p. 15; Tony Gutierrez/AP Images, pp. 16–17; fmua/Shutterstock Images, p. 18; Fred Kfoury III/Icon Sportswire/AP Images, p. 19; Nathan Denette/The Canadian Press/AP Images, p. 20; Red Line Editorial, pp. 21 (timeline), 26; Ken Babbitt/Four Seam Images/AP Images, p. 22; ThePhotosite/Shutterstock Images, p. 23; Elise Amendola/AP Images, p. 27; StefanoT/Shutterstock, p. 30.

ABOUT THE AUTHOR

Derek Moon is a writer and an avid Stratego player. He lives in Watertown, Massachusetts, with his wife, daughter, and Boston terrier, Rockafowla.